JIMMY, THE DOG IN MY LIFE

It was on a wind-blown promontory of the Cornish coast that the author first encountered Jimmy, and it was here that this half-starved, mangy waif decided to forsake its existence of cadging scraps from picnic parties and pass into possession of a fireside, regular meals and the devotion of two human beings. 'Never,' writes Sir Arthur Bryant, 'was a terrier more a terrier – more challenging, inquiring, restless – than this white, brown-capped, black-spotted, stuggy-tailed piece of fur and spirit that had so unexpectedly invaded and ruthlessly dominated our lives.'

This is the beautifully written story of the dog that came to stay, not only in the home but also in the hearts of Sir Arthur and Lady Bryant.

To all those who have owned a dog whom they loved, the story of Jimmy will have a deep appeal; and to the countless thousands who appreciate the quality of Sir Arthur Bryant's prose this book will require no further recommendation.

JIMMY,

THE DOG IN MY LIFE

by

ARTHUR BRYANT

Illustrated by

DAVID ROOK

COLLINS

8 Grafton Street, London W1

William Collins Sons and Co Ltd
London · Glasgow · Sydney · Auckland
Toronto · Johannesburg

Parts of this story originally appeared in the *Illustrated London News*.

ISBN 0 00 211381 3

First published 1960
This reprint 1985

Made and Printed in Great Britain by
William Collins Sons & Co Ltd, Glasgow

JIMMY was a rough-haired English terrier. He had a snow-white coat which, when brushed and washed, was almost dazzlingly white; large and well-proportioned brown and black spots, a short, stuggy brown-tipped tail that usually, like his aspiring spirit, pointed perkily upwards; long, graceful legs that with his stout heart could carry him swiftly as any deer or racehorse; two satiny brown ears that sometimes lay in repose and at others pointed upwards like the pavilions of a mediaeval army; and the most beautiful brown eyes I have ever seen. He may not have conformed to the pedantic requirements of any Breeding Society but, viewed purely as dog, he had everything proper about him.

He entered my life on a Cornish cliff eighteen years ago. It was at the darkest moment of the war soon after our defeat at Knightsbridge and when the victorious Germans were hammering on the gates of Alexandria and Stalingrad, when the position at sea was more grave than at any time of the war and when the Japanese tide in the Pacific and South-East Asia had still to be turned. I had just been given a fortnight's respite from work which I was doing for the Services, and had taken the opportunity of spending ten days in a farmhouse on the North Cornish cliffs. It was my one wartime holiday and during the afternoons my wife and I made the most of it; sometimes picnicking on the beach and at other times taking long tramps over the cliffs. On one of these we walked to Boscastle, about six or seven miles from the farmhouse where we were staying. And there we encountered the waif who for the next fourteen years was to dominate our lives. In a backwater of immeasurable quiet—the quiet of long rollers and surge and heather cliffs—the dog in our lives found us.

We were eating sandwiches at the time on a small promontory overlooking the west side of the harbour, and I had thrown a few crumbs to some gulls who were obviously old *habitués* of the place and who, voraciously soaring and diving, were taking their customary toll of the picnicking few—honeymoon couples, old people and Service men and women on leave who were scattered about the cliff.

Suddenly I became aware that my wife and I were no longer alone. Sitting very silent and intent by our side was a white, shaggy terrier with brown cap and ears and a stump of a tail, gazing at my sandwiches with a look of infinite reproach and longing; he was obviously grieved that such largesse should be distributed among undeserving seagulls. Though food in those days was not plentiful and I was hungry, I was unable to resist the look in those large brown eyes, and my last two sandwiches, bit by bit, were handed over to this obviously expert and, as it turned out, professional beggar. What was so remarkable was that, though, as we subsequently came to realise, he must have been half starving, he made not the slightest attempt to snatch the proffered food and took it so gently that it seemed to leave one's hand by an imperceptible process of suction. Never in all my experience had I known a dog with such a soft mouth or with more gentle winning manners—not even the great-hearted, graceful, deep-ruffed Alsatian who for seven years formed the background to my life and after his death left it, for many months, desolate. This soft mouth was one of the dog's distinguishing traits and always remained so. A connoisseur of food, especially as we discovered later, of the rarer and more expensive kinds, he was never greedy. He merely showed, as only he could, that he needed it, and then waited patiently for his need to be satisfied.

Owing to his half-starved condition, he seemed at the time to be an old dog: thin, matted, mangy, with a pink

hairless underneath on which black spots showed like skin eruptions. We took him to be the property of some poor family who could afford him little food or attention. Yet before he had been with us many minutes he gave us a taste of his quality. A hundred feet or so beneath us was an estuary, with scores of gulls resting on the sand. These the dog obviously regarded as enemies, for he suddenly jumped up, dashed down the precipitous rocks and, barking wildly, drove them, squalling and wheeling, out to sea. Then he raced up the cliff to us, wagged his little stern ecstatically as he approached, and sat down again by our side, intently and wistfully surveying the sandwich-box. The whole exercise was carried out in double-quick time and evinced the highest degree of alertness, zest and *savoir-faire.* And yet, as I have said, he seemed an old, rugged, undernourished dog, and was unquestionably very mangy.

It was only after we had sat there for an hour that we realized with a shock that he had no collar and that he belonged to none of the picnicking parties who had been sharing the promontory with us. And when, now alone, we rose to leave, the dog rose and followed us. Or, to be precise, he preceded us, for from the start of our association he took the initiative. He did so in a manner that made it perfectly clear that there was now a bond between us and that he regarded us as his property. Whenever we paused he paused, and when we sat down —which we deliberately did to see what would happen

—he sat down too, and regarded us with a look of deep interest and affection. He seemed, indeed, for all his shaggy and disreputable appearance, the soul of amiability, for we noted particularly the friendliness with which he greeted the dogs in the outskirts of the little town through which we had to pass, wagging his tail in a frenzy of welcome at their approach and lavishing upon them those attentions which seem to endear dogs to one another. There was never the faintest hint of a fight in his manner; he positively loved his fellow-dogs, all of them, the motion of his quivering tail seemed to say. Not even the churliest cur could have picked a quarrel with a creature so imbued with the spirit of universal charity.

After that, passing through the town, we lost him—or rather, he lost us. We were relieved, for the prospect of a stray dog on our hands so far from home, and at such a time, naturally dismayed us. But some days later, just before my brief holiday ended, we walked over the cliffs again to pay our last visit to the storm-battered estuary where we had encountered the little creature. In the intervening days we had sometimes spoken of him and his inexplicable charm, and had half-wondered whether we should ever see him again. But we were not thinking of him at all when, just as we were finishing our tea in the local hostelry, we found him once more sitting quietly by our side.

It was inevitable, I suppose, that we should have offered him cake, and inevitable, too—though we were not expecting it—that he should again have followed us. This time, as we climbed the steep hill out of the town, it became clear that he was following us in earnest. Remembering that we had a six or seven miles' walk over the cliffs before us, and that we should have to retrace our steps next day—our last before I returned to my labours—if we were not either heartlessly to abandon him or adopt him for life, we were greatly distressed. We were still on a main road, and to all the people we met walking towards the town we explained our plight and asked them to take the dog back to where he belonged. But from them we also learned what we had guessed—that he belonged to nowhere; that he was an inveterate runaway for whom the police were seeking a home and who had been eking out a summer's existence rabbiting on the cliffs and begging largesse from picnic parties. And though two or three of them did their best to lure him back to the town, he refused to be caught and persisted in following us.

A mile or so out of the town our way left the main road and struck across the cliffs. After that, we knew, we should meet no other travellers. We accordingly did our best to persuade the dog to return. But he appeared to regard our gestures and pointings as a species of game, cocked up his ears and watched us for a time, then lost interest and sat down, awaiting our pleasure. In the end I was reduced to threatening him with a stone, which I threw, miserably and feebly, in his direction. When the dog realized that what I was doing was no game, but a deliberate attempt to get rid of him, the confidence in his bearing vanished in a moment and he became a broken, forlorn, abject creature, with drooping tail and tragic eyes. He slunk away, and we hurriedly resumed our path towards the cliff; daring neither to speak nor look at one another. I felt as though I was a murderer.

But we had not done with the dog; that loving heart was to redeem us. For suddenly my wife gripped my arm and said, "Look," and, turning, I saw him following, miserably, far back from the underside of the hedge. That was the end or, so far as we were concerned, the beginning. We let him come up and thereafter he took charge of us, trotting on ahead of us as though everything was now arranged, as indeed—though we did not know it—it was. But, as we discussed him, I agreed that, if the farmer and his wife with whom we were lodging would let him stay for the next two nights—our last in Cornwall—I would telephone the police in the morning and offer him a home.

At the farm we were successful in obtaining permission for the dog to stay with us. When, after eating our supper, we returned to the room where we had left him on the floor, we found him, to our horror, curled up on one of our landlady's armchairs. It was symptomatic of what was to come: the quiet assurance of it, the luxurious comfort, the air of full proprietorship. Consigned for the night to a barn into which he was inveigled with a bowl of bread and milk—a dish for which, for all his recent hunger, he showed considerable contempt—he was waiting at the door to be let out when early next morning my wife went to release him. I can still see that eager, slightly offended, little white figure emerging like a bullet from his place of confinement and greeting his rescuer on the top of the stone steps that led to it.

During that day the dog was constantly disappearing and reappearing, as befitted the incorrigible rover he so clearly was. And yet the curious thing was that, just as he took food so gently and with such irreproachable manners, he was perfectly house-trained. In all the fourteen years he was with us, only once did he misbehave himself in a house, and then in the staircase hall of an immense nineteenth-century Gothic edifice whose pillars he not unnaturally confused with lamp-posts. A good home he must have had at some time, and now he apparently wanted another. And yet in all other ways he was a wild dog, used to complete liberty and impatient of the slightest restraint. In the course of the morning, while we were bathing, he attached himself to at least half a dozen other parties, and there seemed no reason to expect that he would remain with us. When I telephoned the police to offer him a home he had already vanished, only to reappear unexpectedly soon after the permission to take him had been granted.

Yet when that afternoon, after we had toiled up the cliff from the beach after his twentieth disappearance and my wife and I had agreed that if he rejoined us, as at that moment he did, I should walk him back to Boscastle and return him there if he would follow me—since it scarcely seemed a kindness to deprive one of his liberty who valued it so much—he turned his back firmly on me and persisted in following his mistress to the farm and a life of domesticity. He had chosen.

Next morning, when the car called to take us to the station, he had again disappeared—rabbiting—and it seemed certain we should have to depart without him. But just as the luggage was being put in, he reappeared. My wife had made him a collar of string, and with this round his neck—a symbol of his changed status—he accompanied us to the station. When he saw the train and realized he was to go with us he went mad with joy. And through all the long, crowded journey to London he remained quiet and gentle, curled up at our feet or in the corridor, patiently awaiting his future. Even Waterloo, with its to him bewildering turmoil and clatter, did not daunt that staunch little heart, though when a little later his mistress left the taxi and disappeared into a shop he became wildly agitated. And when, late at night, we arrived after further train and car journeys at the old North Buckinghamshire house that for the next three years was to be his home, he trotted into the garden as though he had lived there all his life. By every muscle of his taut, alert body he made it clear that he regarded it as his own.

* * *

From an existence of rabbit-hunting on wind-blown

cliffs, cadging scraps out of paper bags from picnic parties and periodic sojourns in village police stations, Jimmy, as we christened him, passed into the possession of nearly all that a stray dog can ask—a fireside, regular meals, regular petting, soft sitting and lying and the devotion of two human beings. Within twenty-four hours of his arrival, despite some foolish talk by his new owners about housing him in an outhouse, he had established himself on his mistress's bed, which remained his sleeping place until he died fourteen years later. It was astonishing how quickly he changed from the gentle, almost barkless creature we had found into an animal almost embarrassingly vocal, with the lordliest airs and a pugnacity towards every creature bigger than himself that would have done credit to a Red Indian on the warpath. He became, at once, a boss dog, and let the world know it. Never was terrier more a terrier—more challenging, inquiring, restless—than this white, brown-capped, black-spotted, stuggy-tailed piece of fur and spirit that had so unexpectedly invaded and now so ruthlessly dominated our lives. If he felt his authority and superiority to the rest of his species to be challenged in even the smallest particular, he gave loud and authoritative tongue and prepared to fight. No Tammany Hall boss, no European dictator could be more insistent and menacingly urgent about his rights and powers. In his own esteem, he was the first dog in any place into which

he entered and, regardless of questions of size and dog-power, was ready to force any possible challenger to admit it. Nor did he wait for challengers. He looked round for them and joyfully invited them.

Yet—and this was the pathos of him—a harsh word, a stick raised to chasten, a suitcase packed for a journey he might not share, and all the confidence went out of him like water drained from a cup. His tail went down, his head hung, and a look of unutterable sadness came into his big, brown eyes. Even chocolate, which in some mysterious way—and most inconveniently, seeing it was stringently rationed—he made it clear he loved above all other foods, would remain untouched at his feet if his mistress went out without him. To her, for all his fiery challenge to a world which had tragically misused him and which he had now so triumphantly overcome, he gave a love as single-hearted and unquestioning as I have ever witnessed in any creature, human or animal.

Jimmy's first three years of domesticity were wartime years. They must have seemed to him strangely static. His master, doing work for all three Services, was often away, travelling by rail, road and sometimes by air, while Jimmy remained with his mistress in the heavy clay Buckinghamshire uplands. I think he regarded this as a real deprivation, for all his life he was essentially a dog who wanted to be off somewhere. It mattered little to him where, so long as he went, and up to the end any journey, even the shortest—for a shopping expedition or merely to take the car a hundred yards to the garage at the back of the house—was heralded by excited, imperious barking.

Having no outlet for his roving instincts at a time when unnecessary journeys were frowned on, not only for little dogs but for non-combatant humans, he at this period of his life frequently, and not unnaturally, ran away. It was not that he wanted to leave us; on the contrary, from the start he was clearly as devoted to us as we were to him and always returned to us with every manifestation of passionate devotion and contrition for having left us. But he could not resist his longing for adventure. We had only to leave a window or the garden gate open and he would be through it and, though at first he might intend to go no further than the neighbouring smallholder's manure heap—our village dogs' club—or to pick a bone, in more senses than one, with his great enemy and rival, Farmer Hinton's dog down the road, unless speedily detected and recalled he would as likely as not attach himself to some passing soldier or follow a scent across the fields and, travelling at his usual remarkable speed—for he could outdistance a bicycle coasting down the steepest hill—soon be far beyond recall or, in those petrol-less days, discovery. There would then follow hours of agonized searching the neighbouring fields and woods and, when the searching proved vain, as it almost invariably did, much telephoning to distant police-stations, whence, usually long after nightfall, he would be retrieved by his long-suffering mistress on a bicycle.

On one of his odysseys, I remember, he had followed a W.A.A.F. on a bicycle to a nearby town. Here he spent some hours in the typists' room at the Headquarters of the local Group of Bomber Operational Training Command, being petted and fed on sweet biscuits and other favourite and, at that time, rare foods. Then, feeling the call of the road again or possibly being ejected by outraged higher authority, he transferred himself to an airfield a few miles distant, where, apparently rabbiting, he was caught in the slipstream of a departing Wellington and was subsequently, dazed and much shaken by his aeronautical experience, all but run over by a car. At this point—it was about tea-time and he had been absent since breakfast—we succeeded in picking up his trail as a result of telephoning the entire neighbourhood, including our most august neighbour, the Air Vice-Marshal himself, who, as a result of a kindly search signal, was able to give us a report of his adventures. But he had by then again vanished and it was not till nine o'clock that a police station seven miles away telephoned to inform us that he was once more among his old friends, the constabulary. When collected, at the expense of a week's precious petrol ration, he was found in a circle of solemn policemen beside the station fire, sitting there with an expression of great intelligence and listening to a lecture on gas, though his contentment may have arisen less from his enjoyment of this intellectual fare than from a justly founded association of uniforms with meals and titbits. Yet, as usual, he greeted his rescuers with frantic delight, and returned home, barking, as though reunion with us had been his only thought all day. On this occasion we were so relieved to get him back safe and sound that we had not even the heart to reproach him.

More usually he was punished for his escapades. This usually took the form of a horrible penance called "Black Hole", in which he was banished, amid minatory noises, to a woodshed or cupboard and left there for ten minutes, half an hour or even longer, according to the heinousness of his crime and the degree of exasperation aroused by his misbehaviour. This was a very real punishment for a dog who lived every moment of his time with so great an intensity of feeling. I can still see the look of dejection and shame with which, at the dread words, "Black Hole!" he would creep to his place of captivity. Nor, once there—for he was the manliest of beasts—did he ever howl or try to escape, but remained, a picture of inconsolable dejection, with his head on the ground or pressed miserably against the door until his cruel punishment was over. Meanwhile his jailers suffered quite as acutely as he, as they reflected on his misery and loneliness, until even his inexorable master could bear the thought of his imprisonment and the reproaches of the dog's tender-hearted mistress no longer, and hurried, with ill-concealed eagerness, to let him out. Usually it took several minutes of petting before the dog's self-confidence could be restored and he became once more his eager, assured self.

For under the self-confidence and even arrogance that the possession of a home had given him was the remembrance of what it was to be unloved and homeless. The fierceness and arrogance of his challenge to his fellow-dogs derived, I am sure, from the time when he slunk, a sad, bedraggled little outcast, past farms the savour of whose good things was guarded by a proud, angry house-dog and utterly forbidden to the likes of him. To his dying day I do not believe Jimmy ever lost this deep-seated realization. It made the bond between him and those who had given him a home stronger than the usual bond between dog and man, and anything that seemed to threaten it struck at the roots of his being. I shall never forget the look of terror that came over him once when, hunting on a roadside heath during a halt on a car journey far from his home and familiar haunts, he had to be recalled by the sound of the horn: the fear that we would go without him and condemn him once more to a life of solitary wandering made him suddenly forget, in that agonized moment, even the presence of imminent rabbits. And on another occasion, when he had been taken to a London dog-shop to be clipped and had been left, perhaps injudiciously, to be called for, he was found two hours later as if shell-shocked, unable for a while to take his bearings or know where he was.

* * *

Jimmy had two other great pastimes—the chase and fighting. From running away he was gradually weaned, though it proved a painful process for all, until in the end his odysseys seldom went further than slipping out of one or other of the gates of the great walled garden of his post-war Dorset home, which, because of his weakness, were ordained to be kept permanently shut, and trotting up to the bailiff's cottage to have a snuffle round with his spaniel. But hunting remained his passion to the end, which was natural for a dog who before he found a home and a master had had to support himself by catching rabbits and other wild things on the Cornish cliffs. It was his misfortune that the master he had adopted was without even the most elementary of sporting instincts and hunted nothing at all, unaccountably spending much of the day scribbling on bits of paper—an activity the dog clearly resented and deplored though he gradually came to accept it as inevitable. A "tweedy" master would have suited him far better: the kind of man who, in gaiters and boots, is for ever going out to beat up birds and vermin. With me the entire work of doing so fell on the dog; I did not even possess a gun. Not, perhaps, that an uncontrollably excitable terrier would have been of much use to a gun-keeping master or have been welcomed, or even tolerated, in well-conducted sporting circles.

Because of Jimmy's habit of running away, he was at first given far less opportunity for hunting than would ordinarily have come even a pet dog's way, and his genius in this line was only revealed to his new owners gradually. It was not till he had been with us for several months that he caught his first rabbit, snapping it up during a closely conducted walk with his master as it emerged from a thicket two or three miles from home. Though it was almost half as large as himself he insisted on bearing it back in his mouth like some enormous Victorian moustache, trotting ahead with the gait and pride of a Life Guard on escort duty. Nothing would induce him to put it down or let his master, with base thoughts of supplementing wartime rations, take it from him. His purpose in carrying it, it turned out, was two-fold: first to display it to his mistress and then, this oblation of love made, to bear it off into a private corner of the garden and eat it, very slowly and with much crunching and crackling, all but the tail and ears.

Yet owing to the restrictions of wartime existence and his master's frequent absences from home, few rabbits came the little Nimrod's way during the first three years of his confined domestic existence. His chief sporting outlet in this period of his life lay in our neighbour's manure-heap, always well found with game of a minor kind, and in an old haystack a couple of hundred yards from the house, where his mistress took him for a ramble two or three times every day and where an enormous colony of rats had established themselves. It was so full of them that, when struck with a stick, it quivered and squeaked. Into this, as soon as released from his lead, Jimmy, barking furiously, would shoot like a torpedo, completely disappearing for many minutes while the stack shook and resounded and outraged rats shot out in all directions. How many of his enemies he accounted for in these visitations it was impossible to say, but when at last he emerged and permitted himself to be escorted home it was with bloodstained marks of victory about him, breathless, dusty and almost suffocated with hay seeds. Indeed, as a ratter I have never seen his equal. Some years later, when we were living in a house whose adjoining farm-buildings—separated from it by the exigencies of war and post-war legislation—were so over-run by rats as to become a nuisance, a slightly incredulous Rodent Officer was converted in two dramatic minutes to a full acceptance of our contention by the simple device of letting Jimmy off the lead a hundred yards from a suspected barn and watching him race towards it. He

hurled himself, barking like a machine-gun, against its door, which, when opened, revealed a scene of swirling rodent activity unsurpassed since the days of the Pied Piper and in the course of which Jimmy, admitted at last to a hunting paradise against whose portals he had vainly battered for weeks, accounted for three splendid tuskers in as many seconds.

Twice in his life with us this astonishing hunter, denied the outlet he had enjoyed as a wild stray on the lonely Cornish cliffs, caught a pheasant on the wing, in each case racing at high speed towards it as it sped low across a moor and then leaping high into the air to seize it. But it was not till after the war when the writer took an ancient house and garden left derelict by the Army on the Dorset coast and started to restore them that the dog, as a hunter, came into his own. By this time he must have been eight or nine years old and may even have been more, for we never, of course, knew his exact age. The house had been empty for many months and, being surrounded by what had been a wartime gunnery range and therefore out of bounds to humans, it and its large walled gardens had become a sanctuary for wild animals. When we first saw it there was a large pool of water in the staircase hall under its beautiful Georgian stairs, and one of Jimmy's earliest "bags" was a toad, which to our horror he discovered in this unexpected lacustrine haunt. I say with horror, because we were unaware what it was he had found and, when he suddenly appeared at our side frothing at the mouth, assumed that he had picked up poison and hastily telephoned the nearest vet.

Later, after we had moved into the place, we began to realize what a wealth of sporting opportunities we had unwittingly provided for our fiery little pet. They abounded both inside and outside the house, for while in the garden there were rabbits, squirrels, snakes—including adders—hedgehogs, stoats, badgers and birds innumerable, the interior of the house was rich in animal life of a more domestic kind, mice, rats, bats, toads, as well as plenty of nesting things in the chimneys. And as the gardens had high walls round them and were several acres in extent and as, in the Queen Anne panelling of the room in which we usually sat, there was a little trapdoor about eighteen inches high leading into the garden through which Jimmy was free to wander at will whenever he chose, even our sedentary, unsporting life came for a time to offer all that a dog could desire. He would be in and out fifty times a day, disappearing for long periods from sight except, perhaps, for an ecstatic little tail, as he burrowed in the wilderness at the foot of the garden after a distracting and never-failing variety of living things. And at night as we sat reading by the great bolection-moulded marble fireplace, he would sit, intent, by a mousehole in a corner of the panelling with his head cocked on one side, awaiting with the utmost patience the emergence of the "pitter-pats", as we mutually called them, whom he well knew were only a few inches away. Occasionally he would breathe heavily into the hole to make them more aware of his presence and encourage them to come into the open. Yet once he had retired for the night, satiated after the long day's sport, he insisted on a close season; on one occasion when his mistress was awoken in the night by a mouse investigating a biscuit box on her bedside table, Jimmy's only reaction, when awoken, was a sleepy stare at this after-hours intruder, whom at any other time he would have snapped up instantly.

Gradually, as we mastered the wild and the garden was transformed into trim-cut lawns and borders, the opportunities for hunting within the domain dwindled and the garden lost its interest for Jimmy. Fortunately by then he was growing old and was content to lie in the sun watching his master's unaccountable and apparently useless activities with paper and pencil. But walks on the downs behind the house remained a perpetual delight, for the place swarmed with rabbits, and when the summit was reached and the whole of Dorset, the Isle of Wight and half the Channel were spread out in panorama before a little dog and his master, the former would throw his head back with joy as he inhaled the air—so reminiscent of the Cornish cliffs of his youth—and then race away among the gorse bushes and bracken slopes to hunt to his heart's content. Sometimes, among the burrows, he would start a hundred rabbits, and even as he grew old, "shorter in wind as in memory long" and straight pursuit was no longer availing, he would now and then unexpectedly catch a rabbit as it ran, in the general pandemonium, straight into his mouth. A true sportsman, he always gave warning of approach and when in pursuit often missed his prey owing to his chivalrous habit of barking as he drew near the rabbit's tail, thus causing a diminution of his own pace and an additional stimulus to his quarry. Nor would he take advantage of an enemy's misfortune; on one occasion when on a walk he found a rabbit in an iron trap, he stopped short, turned the other way and solemnly watched his unsporting master release the poor beast, making not the least attempt to pursue it as it hobbled away into the undergrowth.

As for himself, he was always game even when, as sometimes happened, his eagerness led him into trouble.

There was one dreadful time when he unaccountably vanished during an evening walk in a wooded park. After an hour trying to solve the mystery of his disappearance, it occurred to his master that he might have got trapped inside a tree; and, sure enough, after an anxious examination of the bases of a number of ancient oaks, a small palpitating black nose was discovered peeping out of a tiny aperture in the hole of a twisted oak. The dog had obviously entered from a larger hole on the other side, but had been unable to turn, and but for our fortunate discovery would have died a horrible death imprisoned in the tree. While his mistress lay outside the hole whispering encouraging words to the panting little captive within, his master hurried home to arouse the neighbours, who presently arrived with spades, axes and picks. Yet when their efforts were at last crowned with success and an apparently exhausted dog emerged through the exit they had so laboriously enlarged, he immediately raced round to the hole by which he had entered and plunged in again!

Even in London, where much of the second half of his long life was spent, Jimmy succeeded in finding game. Against the cats and pigeons who made use of the small back-garden behind his metropolitan home he waged an incessant, spirited war, rushing downstairs and along a slippery corridor to the door of the room which opened on to this small paved pleasaunce whenever he scented a roving pussy below, and throwing himself against it until it was opened, after which he would dash into the garden like a rocket, barking furiously. Once in his old age, when his mistress returned late and awoke him from his mournful sleep on her bed for his wonted good-night visit to the garden, he broke a leg through the eagerness with which, after flying downstairs, he flung himself at the garden door before there was time to open it.

As for Hyde Park, which happily for him was only a hundred yards from his London home, it abounded, in his belief, in game of a kind, even though every other dog in the place was unaware of its existence. There were no rabbits in the Glen in those early post-war years, otherwise he would certainly have found a way to get through the railings and be after them; but one summer he discovered that the fenced-in space at the eastern end of the Serpentine contained a nest of rats, and every morning he would wade or swim round the railings at the end and spend a few minutes barking and digging ferociously until we were able to retrieve or coax him out. And he persisted in believing that a venerable elm

stump at the edge of the old Exhibition Ground was a repository of mice, despite all evidence to the contrary. As for His Majesty's ducks, we were never quite sure that he might not make a dive at one as it waddled unsuspecting across his path and had to guard carefully against such treasonable activities. On more than one occasion we were only just in time to avert a grievous civic crime.

But Jimmy's more usual London offence was fighting. In his earlier days in the Metropolis, for all our efforts to prevent him, he repeatedly broke the King's peace. Like Winifred Letts's "Tim", he was "a massacree dog that knew no fear" and trailed his coat everywhere. He loved fighting dearly and, with any dog larger than himself, would engage at the slightest provocation. His mistress, who detested such warfare, scarcely dared to let him off the lead in the Park and, when she did, was repeatedly a participant in scenes of the most distressing violence and uproar.

He enjoyed a greater liberty with his master, who as a result of much painful effort—painful for both dog and master—had managed to instil some imperfect degree of obedience into an animal who, after his early life of freedom, had not, at first, even an elementary idea of what obedience meant. Yet though as a result his master could walk him through the Park without a lead, it was only at the price of ceaseless vigilance and much explosive shouting that this little universal challenger could be halted before he hurled himself on his selected prey. Left to himself, he would race towards some other dog spied from afar—the larger the better—and, if the other animal showed the slightest sign of opposing him or of resenting his one-sided approaches, he would take it as a mortal insult, bare his terrifying fangs and set about the unaccommodating stranger. When this occurred, which in his younger days it usually did if I relaxed my watch on him for an instant, old ladies, whose darlings he had insulted and attacked, would shake their umbrellas at me as I arrived, breathless and hoarse, at the scene of the encounter. Gradually as he became more accustomed to urban life, his manners became more civilized, and I could then usually trust him to refrain from fighting, provided I pretended not to notice him and called him, sharply and categorically, at the precise moment when my doing so gave him the chance to end the encounter without loss of dignity—a matter which was obviously of immense importance to him. Provided the other dog was prepared to accept the fact that the bristling exchange of compliments was now at an end, a gradual and stately withdrawal took place, after which, following a valedictory and exceedingly high tilt of the leg, he would rejoin me at a brisk pace.

All this may give a false impression of Jimmy and suggest that he was an ill-tempered dog. Yet, provided his dignity was not affronted, he was the most friendly of creatures and would wag his stern ecstatically at any dog or human he liked. He never attacked a dog smaller than himself or, indeed, anything like as small, for under his beautiful coat of soft, white, curly fur was a little chap no bigger than a small lamb. It was several years after he joined us before we discovered how small, but one hot summer, having sent him to be plucked, I could scarcely believe my eyes when I called for him after the operation. He appeared only half his wonted size and, looking at him with wonder and pity, it shamed me to think of how angrily I had often rebuked his heroic pugnacity and, on occasion, chastised him. Towards all puppies he was long-suffering and gentle, and his anger, I think, was only aroused when he felt that the place he had so suddenly acquired in the universe—that of an important and cherished dog, with all the favours and privileges showered on him by an adoring master and mistress—was being challenged; then he was instantly up in arms.

Once—it was only a year or two after his roving days ended—we took him to stay in a Welsh farmhouse where thirteen farm-dogs were kept. The memories that this clearly aroused in him made our departure in the morning and our return at night a major military operation. It could only be effected at all by one of us carrying him forcibly while the other kept off the insulted farm-dogs, at whom, struggling to be free, he continuously barked a ferocious challenge. That he would have taken on the lot had we allowed him, whatever the consequences, I have not the slightest doubt. Turning tail was not in Jimmy's nature; when a huge bull-mastiff—a notorious fighter—once unexpectedly set on him from behind and all but killed him before he could be made to relax his grip, the little terrier, blinded and torn, rushed back at the aggressor and, had he not been prevented, would have fought to the death. Nor did the experience which all but proved fatal deter him from his perennial readiness for battle. Only age, and the growth of tolerance that came with age, did that.

* * *

Many of my memories of Jimmy are London memories, for much of my time had to be spent there. I used to walk him on summer afternoons to the bandstand, crossing the Park amid a barrage of angry barking and crude canine insults. When we arrived I would take out my letter-case and, under the lovely green of the chestnuts, write while the dog lay at my feet or, if there were few other auditors, sit on a chair beside me looking like Dog Toby in his ruff. It was not much fun for him, for unless I kept him on the lead he would be halfway across the Park after some distant dog before I could write a line. Yet when the fare was provided by a Highland Regiment and there was a sword dance, his look of boredom would change to intense alertness and he would try to follow the Highlanders on to the platform, barking in an ecstasy of pleasure during their display which he seemed to regard as a kind of dog-fight. There was also the satisfaction of straining at his lead and insulting passing members of his species, and, at the end, the still greater satisfaction of leaving the place, which he expressed so audibly that I always had to remain till the close of any piece of music, however much I might dislike it. My wide acquaintanceship with trombone and piccolo solos is almost entirely due to this.

One episode in Jimmy's London life sticks particularly in my memory. It occurred four years before his death, just before old age began to take the fire out of him. It was the morning of Queen Elizabeth's proclamation, and he and I were walking in Hyde Park. Suddenly there was a detonation, causing Jimmy to swerve from his path among the trees of Rotten Row. Having recovered himself, he looked up at me as though to enquire whether some active expression of fidelity and devotion was demanded. Then the detonation was repeated and he jumped again. This time, however, he did not allow it to pass unanswered, and, after a moment's pause, barked back, though still a little uncertainly. Then the gun fired again, and this time he jumped forward defiantly, as a terrier does when challenged, raised his small, resolute head and barked loudly. A duel then began between the invisible gunners and the dog, each mechanical explosion being followed by a canine one of growing ferocity. This continued all the way down the Row, and no threats or entreaties on my part would make him desist. By this time we had left the Row and were crossing the Park in the direction of the firing. As we came up through the still, wintry mist towards the high ground beyond the Serpentine, we saw, first the flashes of guns and then the gun detachments of the King's Troop standing around their guns. And at that moment a most beautiful thing happened. Without a word spoken, and with the most exquisite skill and alacrity, the gun teams galloped forward out of the mist and halted by the guns. Then, before I could recover from my surprise, the guns were limbered up, and the six teams started once more to gallop, now with the guns and the gunners behind them. In a great sweep, and still without any sound but the thud of flying hooves on the grass, they made off westwards across the empty centre of the Park, towards Lancaster Gate, and then swung round northwards and eastwards until they vanished from sight behind the trees of Marble Arch. It might have been Mercer's Battery—"Left limber up and as fast as you can!"—galloping into the inferno of smoke and heat on the ridge at Waterloo. Though, unlike his master, Jimmy was no reading dog, but a simple, fighting one, some such thought may have passed through his mind, for in a flash he was after the guns. But, being an old dog, he presently realized that he could not catch them up, and returned, wagging his tail, his duty done. A few years earlier, he would have followed them into the Edgware Road and probably laid hold of a gun!

In a sense that protest against England's artillery was prophetic, for a few months later a tragedy happened in Jimmy's life. Hitherto his happiest moments, and mine, had been when we set off for the country together: to that other home, furnished with rabbits, rats, well-populated ricks and haystacks, compost-heaps and everything a sporting dog could require to fulfil his destiny. When such moments came and the long railway or motor journey was over, and the car climbed the steep slope of the rabbit-haunted Purbeck hills, a chant of exultation would break from that quivering throat. It was a kind of royal proclamation to all the vermin for miles round to take precipitately to their burrows or suffer the worst! But a shadow now fell on all this happiness and bravado—a shadow of inexplicable terror and anxiety. For this uncontrollable little dog, once a silent and haunted-looking stray, was not the only maker of noise in the green and tawny vales between the limestone hills and the dark cliffs of shale where his hunting paradise lay. Beyond the chalk ridge on the horizon, mysterious monsters lurched and slithered about a sandy wilderness of little heathy hills, discharging their detonating missiles from long, thin shafts as they practised incessantly for the next—or perhaps, in keeping with age-long military tradition, the last—war to end war. And, having for years treated heavy artillery with the fearlessness with which he normally treated every manifestation of man or nature, Jimmy one August day reacted to the morning's first shots from the Bovingdon Gunnery Range with a display of fear that no one had ever witnessed in him. Instead of ignoring them as he had always done, or boldly barking back at them as he had done to the guns in the Park, he gave one terrified look and fled to the coal cellar. A few minutes later, covered with coal dust, he emerged and, panting with anxiety, started to circle round my legs. All day, while the bombardment lasted, he continued to alternate between furious digging and scrabbling in cupboards and dark corners, and trotting, like a crazy automaton, round me. Work became virtually impossible, for, apart from the agony of seeing a beloved friend in such a plight, whenever I started to settle myself to my task, he would fling himself into my lap and lie there panting and trembling, until out of sympathy I found myself trembling too. If I moved to fetch a book or folder of notes, he would run in circles between my legs, bringing me more than once to the ground. Nor would the poor animal, usually so full of intelligence and sensitivity and eager for every pleasurable experience, pay the slightest attention to the familiar heralds of his wonted treats; the sight of his lead and the magic word "walk"; the opening of the sacred tin in which his chocolates lived and before which he would often lie, like a Trafalgar Square lion, for hours at a stretch, growling at every unlicensed person who approached; the rattle of keys that announced the opening of the car in which he so loved to ride. Nothing could comfort him or restore him to consciousness of anything but the ungovernable terror riding through his poor, crazed mind. Occasionally, when the guns became temporarily silent, he would recover sufficient composure to creep up from the cellar, bedraggled and ashamed of himself, and lie miserably in a corner, listening for the dreaded sound. And next morning he was listening apprehensively even before they began. The moment they did so, the same manifestations of terror occurred. After a day or two we took him away.

Thereafter Jimmy's pleasure in the country never returned. Nothing seemed to avail against the terror which the guns, reverberating among the Purbeck hills, aroused in him. The secret of his fear—so pathetic to behold—seemed to lie in some cause beyond our curing; perhaps in some episode in his now remote and, to us, unknown youth. And watching him listening intently for the cruel thunder to begin beyond the encircling hills, and trying to comfort and reassure him, it was not hard to guess what that memory might have been. It was something that must have happened to many a bewildered dog in England's blitzed cities: the roaring from the skies, the shaking streets and houses, the sudden and disintegrating thunder and fire that, in a flash and cascade of falling masonry and rubble, robbed a little creature, with as great a capacity for love and fidelity as any human, of all it had known and loved. And I suspect that it may have been that memory that caused Jimmy, as he lay cowering in the cellar to emerge every few minutes from his shelter and hurry, shuddering and trembling, into the room where his foolish master, disregarding all warnings, sat at his work, to assure himself that he was still alive and to implore him to take shelter before the tragedy of his youth was re-enacted.

* * *

It is all so long ago now that it is difficult to recreate Jimmy as he was in his early days before age and trouble came to him. I recall rather the years of dignity and consequence, when he had no need to assert himself and had become the admired friend of all who knew him—the central figure of two homes, a host to all visitors, particularly those who came to dinner and whose arrival he anticipated by working himself into a prophetic frenzy of excitement despite every attempt to keep him quiet, a familiar and honoured figure in Hyde Park and on the roads of Purbeck, which he travelled seated, or rather standing, on his master's knee, barking imperiously at everyone and everything who it seemed to him stood in need of barking at and occasionally flying over the back seat, still barking, to complete the discomfiture of some bewildered wayside dog whom he had singled out for this mark of his passing displeasure. His love of the car grew with the years until it became his favourite spot on earth, dearer even, it seemed to us, than his mistress's bed.

When his insensate terror of gunfire turned his beloved Dorset home into a place of horror, the only comfort we could offer him, until in despair we gave up visiting the place altogether except when the gunners were on holiday, was to hurry him to the car and shut him up in it. Here and here alone he felt safe or comparatively safe. In earlier days, before the car became too decrepit for long journeys, with what joy he esconced himself on top of the luggage at their start before leaping on to his master's knee and pressing his nose against the windscreen while the latter struggled, regardless of a wagging tail in his face, to write an article or memorandum.

Perhaps the most poignant of all memories of this beloved companion is that of the intense anxiety, and, when anxiety gave place to the knowledge that he was not to be left behind, joy with which he set out on journeys. Long before the hour of departure he would have mounted guard on the piled luggage in the hall, passionately resolute not to be left behind. Indeed, as he grew older it became quite impossible to leave home without him. And when train journeys—a far more comfortable mode of travelling with him as companion—succeeded car journeys, with what eagerness, despite old age and infirmity, did he stand in the taxi, swaying on his master's knees as it sped towards Waterloo, and with what tremendous barking, still remembered by the porters there, he entered that station, temporarily drowning every sound in the vast, echoing space but his own triumphant announcement of his coming. That so much noise could come from that minute, frail white form was something of a miracle.

I like to think that at the crack of doom I shall hear that sound again. That inseparable friend of so many years—or rather the casket containing his ashes—lies now beneath the turf of a West Country lawn looking down a valley where Dorset and Wiltshire meet and in whose woods he had often hunted rabbit, fox and badger. Gone are the sad last memories of vet and injection and the growing pain and infirmity of those last years—so bravely and patiently borne. There only remains the recollection of an unquenchable vitality and capacity for life, above all for love and loyalty, and of something which for want of a better word I can only call nobility. True to his nature as a dog—fierce, independent, proud and predatory—he displayed towards the humans who had befriended him a trust, a selfless tenderness and devotion that nothing could alter and which as much as any experience of life, has convinced me that, in some mysterious way beyond our understanding, love is eternal.